THE SPACEFLIGHT SIX

By
JOE PALUMBO

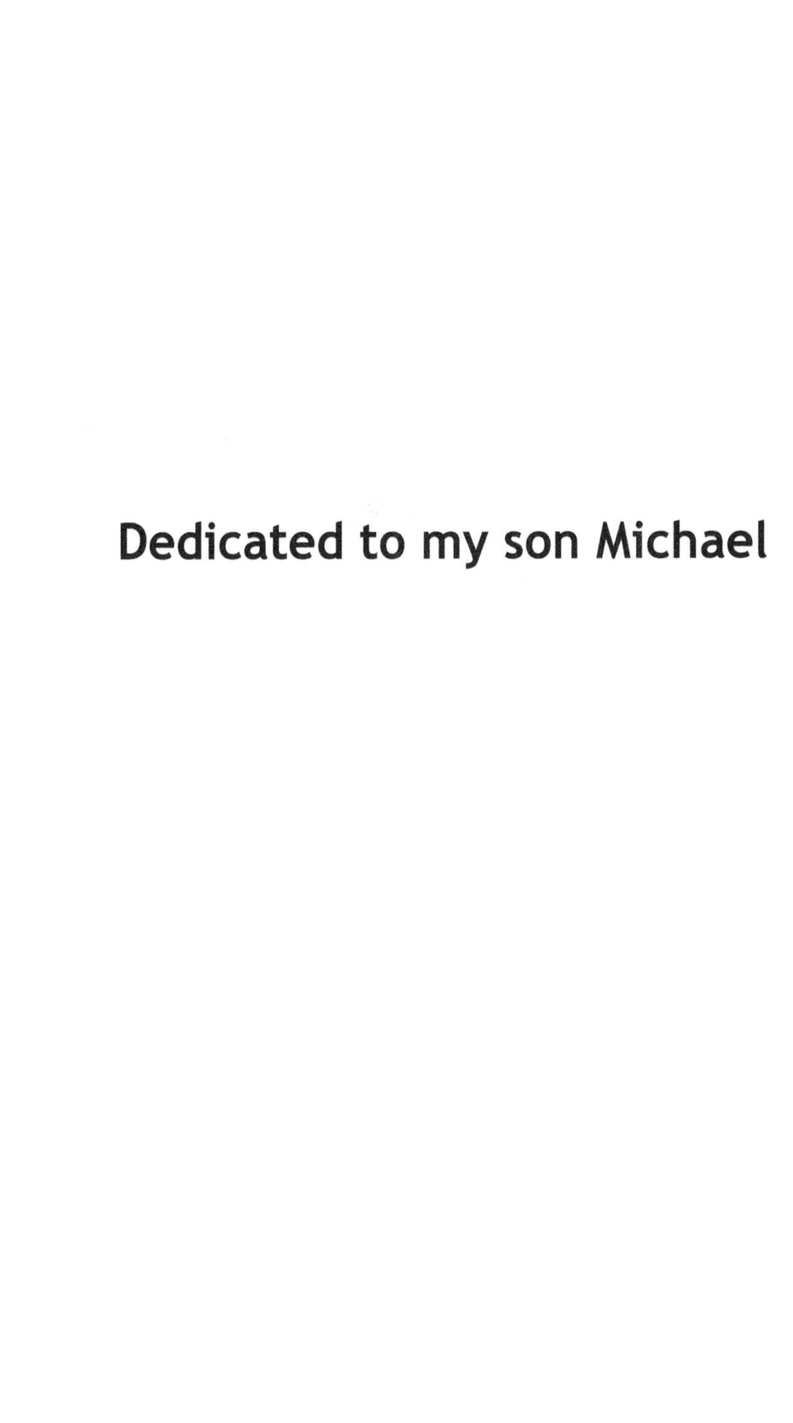

Dedicated to my son Michael

"The sky is the limit only for those
who aren't afraid to fly."

-Bob Bello

Table of Content

Chapter 1

Appleton Science Fair- 2038 the sign held high above the doors to the gym at Appleton Middle School. People were pouring in through the doors. This was the biggest event of the school year. In the corner of the gym sat Brandon Burke going over his notes before the judges came over to his table.

At eleven years old, Brandon was ahead of his time with his science projects. His teachers never knew what to expect from him but they knew his projects would be amazing. This year was no exception. On the table were models of a rocket and satellite that he worked on for the whole year. From afar, his project might not look like much to the naked eye, but Brandon would never make a project so simple. Next to the models was a small laptop accompanied by a small box with a hole in the front. He smiled knowing that the judges would be amazed once they saw his project in action.

He looked around catching a glance of the other students' projects.

"Well, well, well," Brandon heard a voice coming close to his table. "What do we have here, Brandon?"

Brandon rolled his eyes, knowing what was coming next. For as long as he could remember, Ethan always made the Science Fair a competition among the two of them. Brandon did his best with his projects because he loved science, not for the prize of first place.

"Hi, Ethan."

"This is your project?" Ethan cracked up laughing. "You've got to be kidding me!"

"What is it, Ethan? What is wrong with my project?" he looked up at his schoolmate.

"This is what you brought to the fair this year? Models? You can't be serious."

Brandon ignored the question. "What's your entry this year?"

"Much better than this, I can tell you. Come, let me show you," Ethan said.

Brandon hated leaving his project unattended but he had to see what Ethan made this year that made him so confident he'd win first place. He followed Ethan to his table where he saw a volcano on a table sitting beside a pair of virtual reality goggles. "This is it," Ethan proudly smiled.

"This is exactly the same project you had last year," Brandon noted.

"That's where you're wrong," Ethan smiled. "It's not the same as last year's project at all. I improved it with sensory and olfactory components so you can feel like you're standing at a real volcano and feel its effects without getting hurt." Ethan turned around and saw their science teacher standing by his table. "Mrs. Lawson, here put on these goggles and test it out.

The teacher put on the goggles and looked at Ethan waiting for him to start the project. He pressed a button on his laptop and the volcano began to erupt and shoot lava. On the screen, everyone walking by could see what the teacher was seeing through the goggles. "As you can see, the person wearing the goggles is put right into the middle of the volcano and surrounded by the lava and smoke, giving you the feeling of being inside the volcano," he told those checking out his project.

"You aren't kidding, Ethan," Mrs. Lawson said. "I can actually smell the sulfur. And...OUCH!" she jumped. "That felt like the lava is touching my skin."

Suddenly, the goggles started to short circuit and a spark singed her hair. "ETHAN!" the teacher took the goggles off and threw them on the table. "Are you trying to kill me?"

"Mrs. Lawson, I'm so sorry about that." He turned to Brandon and smiled. "Alright, so it needs a little more work. I'm glad I brought a fire extinguisher with me in case something like this happened," he laughed and nudged Brandon.

Brandon shook his head, not cracking a smile. "A little too late for that if you ask me," he told Ethan before walking back to his table as two judges approached.

"Now this is the contestant I was waiting to see today," Clarence Bryant, a judge, turned to Alice Lowery, the second judge. "Alice, this is Brandon Burke I was telling you about. Last year's winner."

"Brandon, I heard so much about you," Alice shook his hand. "Clarence told me that every year you always top your last project."

"Thank you," Brandon blushed. "I try my best."

"Brandon", Clarence spoke. "Please show us what you have brought us for this year's project."

"Sure," Brandon smiled. He turned to his laptop and turned it on. "Play hologram."

Instantly, a beam of light shot out of the box where it showed a hologram of Brandon outside with a twelve-foot rocket behind him on the ground. "Hello," the hologram spoke. "My name is Brandon Burke and this is my entry for this year's science fair. This is my rocket named Major Tom, which comes from the David Bowie song. My dad is a huge fan, but that's another story for another time. Today, it's all about science and exploration of space. This particular rocket runs on food scraps which is easy to get from the cafeteria seeing as many of us students throw the food out instead of eating it."

The judges laughed along with Brandon at his statement. The hologram continued to speak. "The payload is a satellite named X24. The main purpose is to help the economically poor areas and developing countries find hidden groundwater."

Behind the hologram, the rocket took off. "I was given permission to test the rocket here at SpaceX launch facilities in the Mohave Desert. I needed a place that gave me all the space I needed."

The judges' jaws dropped in shock as they watched the hologram. "Excuse me for a moment," Alice said. "Brandon, how old are you again, eleven? How in the world were you able to raise enough money to make the rocket if you don't mind me asking?"

"I received a grant from The National Science Foundation," Brandon smiled. He was about to shut off the hologram when a woman's scream rattled the gym. Everyone turned their head in the direction of the sound.

On Ethan's table, everyone saw a volcano on fire as well as the goggles a judge was wearing. "Hold still," Ethan grabbed the fire extinguisher to put out the goggles. The judge glared at Ethan shaking her head. "ETHAN!" she yelled as he continued to put out the volcano fire. "This is not safe for a Science Fair entry!"

Chapter 2

While chaos was happening at Appleton Middle School, things weren't going much better at Tang Headquarters. Everyone was running around like chickens without heads and it was up to one person to try and pull it all together, Galen Noble. He was a man in his late thirties and normally loved his job at Tang. Days like this were an exception and he wished he was home where he wouldn't have a headache.

What he thought was going to be an easy day at work for once, was no longer an option. When he got the memo from John Lawrence, the CEO of Tang, stating that he had to report to the boardroom immediately, he knew that they received bad news about the company. Minutes after getting the message, Galen found himself sitting at the long table in the boardroom with other executives, all wondering what caused the sudden meeting. It wasn't like John to call them away from their offices without reason.

Everyone was getting antsy waiting for John to enter the room. Galen looked around the boardroom that was full of Tang memorabilia. Tang wasn't popular while he was growing up, but he remembered the first time he tried it. The day his mother brought it home was when he discovered his love for its flavor.

"Can I have your attention," John walked into the boardroom and took his seat. "I just got the latest report for our sales and we have a problem. The thing is, no one under the age of eighty knows what Tang is. They're all into these new drinks that are out on the market. If we don't do something soon to raise our sales, Tang will be history."

Everyone was silent aside from a few mumbles in the room. John turned to Galen, "Galen, we need something that will get the youth of today to connect with Tang. Do you have any idea how we could get that to work?"

There was silence in the room, everyone trying to think of ideas that would work. When he didn't get a response from Galen, John excused himself and walked out of the room. If Tang went down, they would all be out of jobs.

One by one, the executives left the boardroom, heading to their offices to brainstorm. "Galen, hold up!" Jaden Novak called out. "Can we talk for a moment?"

"What is it? Do you have an idea that we should bring up to John?"

Jaden shook his head, "Not at the moment. Know what we need? We need a spark to bring Tang back to the market. If not, then I'm afraid we're all going to be looking for new jobs."

Galen sighed as the two of them continued walking down the hall to their respective offices. "I know. But I didn't hear anyone else come up with suggestions".

*****

That night, after dinner Galen went straight to his home office. He didn't want to waste another moment trying to figure out an idea to bring in front of John the next morning Sitting in front of him were piles of paper with possible ideas but the more Galen looked at them, the more he realized that he hadn't made any progress.

An hour passed and then another, Galen got nowhere. He was staring at the papers and couldn't believe what he saw. John wasn't kidding when he said sales were declining, but Galen didn't expect them to drop at least twenty percent each month. At this rate, Tang would be out of business by the end of the year.

"Plan on coming to bed anytime soon?" his wife, Angela appeared in the doorway.

"Soon," he said going back to his papers. Angela nodded and began to walk away.

"Hold on a moment," he put his finger up. "Angela, tell me; what is one thing the younger generation of today loves?"

"Sleep," she plainly said.

"Besides that. How about Pop-Tarts? He held up a photo of a proposal he made up of a Tang-flavored Pop-Tart. "I was just thinking, what if we teamed up with Kelloggs to create this new flavor?"

Angelina made a face. "I know you mean well, but a Tang-flavored Pop-Tart? I don't think that's a good combination. But don't take my word for it. I'm tired and need some sleep. Ask me again in eight hours, I might have a different opinion on it when I'm more awake."

Galen nodded. "You can go to bed, I'll be there in a few minutes."

He watched his wife leave his office. A few minutes later he got up, shutting off the light. Before heading up to bed, he walked into the kitchen and opened the refrigerator. He looked around and a smile crossed his face. "That's it!"

Chapter 3

Sleep came easy for Galen once he thought of the perfect idea to bring Tang's sales up. It was impossible for this idea not to work. That morning, he arrived at work with a confident attitude that everyone in the boardroom would love his idea.

He arrived in the boardroom before the executives, giving him time to prepare his notes. Nine o'clock came around and the doors opened as the executives piled in. Once everyone was seated, Galen stood up.

"I want to thank everyone for coming here on time," he welcomed the executives, turning on the OLED screen in front of him for all to see. "As we are all aware, yesterday John brought to our attention the falling sales of Tang. I spent all night trying to think of the perfect idea to get the younger generation's attention. You see this smile on my face right now? I'm smiling because I'm extremely excited about my idea. Who knows what the younger demographic enjoys more than anything else in the world?"

"Video games!" Robert Horn said out loud. Everyone in the room chuckled.

"Alright, that's true, Robert. But not the angle I was going for. I'm talking about getting them to want to try and enjoy the taste of Tang. Do you know the energy drink market is an eight-billion-a-year market? And what is Tang? A way to improve your drinks." Galen tapped on the OLED screen, showing a Tang-flavored energy drink. "I'm here to introduce to all of you the Cosmo Boost energy drink, infused with Tang." He could hear the grumbles and he knew he was losing the executives. "Hear me out. This idea takes us back to the days of our founding days and space exploration. What is Tang now? Old and weathered. What does it need? A boost, the same people get when they have an energy drink." Galen smiled and took a seat, waiting to hear the responses from the people in the room.

"I'm not sure, Galen. The market already has more than enough energy drinks. Why would they want to add another one?" John asked. "Any other ideas?"

Galen shook his head and looked down. "I thought of a Tang-flavored Pop-Tart, but that idea sounds even worse than this."

John reached across and patted Galen's back. "You tried and that's better than nothing." He handed him a business card. "Here, take this."

"What's this?" Galen asked looking at the card.

"This is from the company, Core Media. I personally know the CEO of the company and he's always looking for qualified marketing people. Just keep it in mind."

"Thanks," Galen frowned.

*****

Dejected, Galen sat in the living room of his home. He was still upset that his idea was shot down by every single person in the boardroom. He shrugged and turned on the television.

Looking up at the television screen, he turned on the news where they were playing back footage from earlier in the day of a rocket launching off to the International Space Station. Right now, running off and getting lost in space was looking like a great idea to Galen. There he wouldn't be told that his ideas were no good for the company. But here he was, sitting in front of his television feeling defeated.

"Hey, Dad?" Ryan walked into the living room, startling Galen.

"Hey, buddy…. Did you finish your homework?"

"Almost. I was just taking a break to get a snack. What are you watching?" Galen pointed to the television that was replaying the launch once again. "Oh, we saw this in school today. Our teachers had all the students gathered in the auditorium to watch it live. It was amazing to watch it on television."

"I wish I could see a space launch in person," Galen said. "That was always something I dreamt of as a child. Want to come and watch it again with me?" he patted the spot next to him on the couch.

Ryan nodded and sat on the couch next to his father. Galen rewound the news story to the beginning. Father and son watched in amazement as the rocket went off into space. "Space exploration always seems to advance in years in such a smooth manner," Galen noted.

"Are you alright, dad?" Ryan asked.

"Yes, son. There's been a lot of stuff going on at work; it just has me thinking."

They continued to watch the launch when the news story ended and Galen shut off the television. "Know how you said it would be amazing to see a launch in person?" Ryan mentioned.

"Yes, son. What about it?"

"I was just thinking while watching it on TV right now that it would be a cool experience to see the International Space Station up close and in person. I'm sure that would be a dream come true for many kids my age."

Galen nodded and smiled.

"You know what, Ryan? You're right. That would be wonderful." Galen took his son's words to heart. Thanks to his son, he may have the perfect idea to bring to John in the morning.

Chapter 4

The next morning, Galen woke up with an extra spring in his step. He made sure to write down all the notes from the idea Ryan gave him from the night before. Little did his son know that as they watched the news together, he helped him figure out how to get the sales up for Tang. Galen stayed awake until the early morning hours to make sure everything was perfect for his presentation this morning. He didn't want to be turned away like the day before. He wouldn't be able to stand another defeat, for he knew that he found the perfect way to get the younger generation acquainted with Tang.

Galen sat at the head of the table in the boardroom as the executives walked in, the smile on his face never leaving. He was ready for whatever was thrown his way during this meeting. Little did they know that a simple talk with his son brought the greatest idea he ever had since coming to Tang.

Once everyone sat down and settled in, John turned to Galen. "Galen, I'm sure you're ready for your presentation."

"Thank you, John. I'm ready. After a long night, I discovered it's not our product we have to change, but rather how to grab the attention of the younger audience. You were right about the market already being flooded with energy drinks. The last thing they need is a new one coming out. What we need to think about is how do we get publicity and get our product to stand out. And I found the perfect way. He pressed on the OLED screen where an advertisement appeared. **TANG CONTEST: WIN ONE OF SIX TRIPS TO THE INTERNATIONAL SPACE STATION AS A SPACE TOURIST. CONTEST OPEN TO TWEENS BETWEEN THE AGES OF 11-13 ONLY! BUY TANG AND KEEP THE 10-DIGIT CODE UNDER LIDS TO SEE IF YOU ARE A WINNER!!!**

Galen waited for a response and saw as the executives looked unsure about his idea. He turned to John, hoping he had a different reaction.

"Galen, I think your idea is definitely different than anything we ever heard. Would you mind explaining this idea a little more in-depth? I don't think everyone in this room quite understands what it is you're getting at. And why is it only for those between eleven and thirteen? Wouldn't we want to engage more to those higher in their teen years?"

"I think it's better to have the contest winners being young because ISS Chief Director, Lester Jacobs, mentioned four months ago during a press conference that he wished he could research the effects of weightlessness on a developing body, hence tweens who are in the process of their bodies developing. That is exactly the same demographic we're trying to reach, those who are heavily into social media. That's the goldmine. Last night I did research on how we can even bring this contest into existence and I found there is a private space exploration company called Strato-Labs and next year, they plan on bringing people to the ISS. If we get them on board with this contest, they'll be bringing our winners to the ISS."

Bernice began to laugh and soon the other executives joined in. "I'm sorry, Galen, but this really seems like a far-fetched idea you gave us. I'm sure Strato-Labs wouldn't agree to this. Why would they want to risk their reputation with Tang?"

Galen smiled. "That's where you're wrong, Bernice. You see, when I had this idea, I called their CEO, a Mr. Tim Richberg, and he loved the idea. And why wouldn't he? We would call it a dual marketing partnership."

He looked over at John. "What do you think?

"Well, a few things Galen. First, I'm not sure, for legal reasons, we can set up a contest for people that young. Most contests ask for those eighteen or above. Not as young as eleven. Second, I don't know if it's healthy for kids that young to go up into space. And would their parents even agree? It's not like we're sending them to another state or country." He turned to Eric Mathis. "You're part of the legal team, what do you think about this?"

Eric pondered at John's question, tapping his pen on the table. He wasn't expecting to be thrown a legal question out of nowhere during today's meeting. "Well, I'm sure we would give the parents a consent form before allowing them to go out into space. So, I don't see why not. That way, if anything does go wrong, we wouldn't be held responsible since the parents agreed to the terms. And Strato-Labs is a big company, I'm pretty sure they have all the legal problems sorted out since they've already thought about sending people to space. I doubt we'll have any problems when it comes to getting liability insurance for this contest."

"I think the research angle is the best way to go about

it," Sarah added in. "That would give us the legality we need to make this contest happen."

"And the publicity for this contest is going to be outstanding," Galen continued. "Coming from someone who's been working as the marketing director for sixteen years, I can assure you that this is going to eat up all of our yearly advertising and marketing budgets. I know that sounds like a lot, but I give you all my word, it'll be worth every penny. Can you imagine how the sales will sky-rocket? Our returns will be out of this world," Galen laughed at his own puns.

"Alright," John stood. "Honestly, I don't see how this idea won't work. But of course, it's not only up to me to make a decision. Let's take a vote."

"Remember," Galen added. "If we don't think of any other ideas to bring publicity to Tang, we could be out of business much sooner. Please take that into consideration while thinking about your vote."

Sarah and Eric were the first two executives to raise their hands. Galen had no doubt that others would follow suit, considering those who dealt with the legal aspects agreed. Soon, one by one everyone else raised their hands, even Bernice who finally softened at the idea. Galen waited and raised his hand, not wanting to sound too eager about his idea. It all came down to John who had the last say. He looked at Galen's screen once again and nodded. "I like it. I say let's do it!"

Chapter 5

A few days later, Brandon was in his room decorating it with space decals. On the center of his shelf, he displayed his first-place ribbon from the last Science Fair. Everyone loved the rocket he made and they were impressed at his work being advanced for someone so young.

His printer stopped across his room and he walked over to grab the space decals he downloaded off his computer. He climbed up a step ladder placing the decals across his ceiling and smiled at his work. They were glow-in-the-dark and he couldn't wait for night to fall so he could feel as if he was outdoors under the stars without leaving the luxury of his bed.

Brandon finished hanging up the last of the decals when he heard an incoming Skype call coming from his computer. *Wonder who that could be,* he thought, rushing down from the ladder and over to his computer. "Hello?" Brandon didn't recognize the man on the screen or how he got his number.

"Brandon, I'm so glad to have reached you. I'm Tim Farrington from the World Water Organization. I don't know if you heard of us, but we have some good news for you. Your teachers informed us about the satellite you created for your science project and we took a look at it. We are impressed with the results we've been seeing from it. Take a look at these images we have collected from the satellite." Tim flashed photos across the screen of villagers finding wells. "And this was a video sent to us from a group of poor farmers. They wanted to show their thanks by doing this tribal dance in honor of your work."

Brandon smiled. Up until now, he had no idea how much his science projects were helping those in need. "Brandon, as you can see, with your project alone, we were able to help hundreds of people in this village. After all the work and effort we put into finding a way to help them, you were the only one to find a solution. Let me be the first to congratulate you on everything."

"Thank you," Brandon beamed.

*****

Back at Tang Headquarters, everyone was getting ready to launch the biggest publicity event in their history of being a company. Galen had faith that his idea was going to work and bring their sales up to what they once were, but still, he couldn't shake the feeling of dread that sat down deep inside. If this idea didn't work, all the blame would be solely on him. *This has to work. It just has to,* he told himself every morning he went into the office. Currently, everything was running according to plan.

Galen was in his office trying to go over notes before the next conference when there was a knock on the door. "Come in."

"Galen," Jaden walked into his office. "John sent me in here to find out if you sent out the email for the press release."

He nodded as he gathered his notes and walked over to Jaden. "Everything is sent out. Just hope enough people show up for this conference," he took a deep breath.

"What's wrong? Aren't you ready to announce the contest?" Jaden asked.

"As ready as I'll ever be," he sighed.

The two men left Galen's office and headed down the hall to the conference room. "Galen, if you want my opinion, I don't think you have anything to worry about. I know there were a few who didn't think this contest was a good idea, but I have a feeling it's going to get a lot of tweens to enter."

Galen nodded. "I sure hope so. I know if my son was eligible to enter, he would. After all, his interest in going up to space was what gave me the idea for this contest in the first place." He opened the door to the conference room and gestured for Jaden to go in first. "Well, here it goes. No turning back now."

Inside, the room was empty except for the few reporters who sat waiting patiently. *Alright, not that many here today. That's fine. Not going to worry about that now. The other reporters probably think this is a crazy idea and I don't blame them.*

John walked over to Galen and patted him on the back. "Are you ready for this?" he asked.

"I think so," Galen nodded. "Do you think it's a bad sign that not many reporters showed up?"

"I wouldn't worry about that. I'm sure once the contest

is underway, more reporters will want to be part of the conference."

John and Galen took their seats at the table and welcomed the reporters. "Good afternoon everyone. I'm John Lawrence, CEO of Tang. Sitting here next to me is Galen Noble, our Marketing Director. We asked you to come here today as we announce a new and exciting contest we will be running as a partnership with Strato-Labs. This contest will be opened to all those across the globe from ages eleven to thirteen." He turned to Galen, "Want to take it from here?"

Galen nodded. "Tomorrow, starting at seven in the morning, Eastern Standard Time, all Tang products on the shelves will contain a ten-digit Spaceflight Code under the lids. There will be six lucky winners who will receive a chance of a lifetime prize of going up into space on the Strato-Labs' Star Reacher Rocket with the ultimate destination being the International Space Station."

Galen turned to John to end the press conference. "The winners will be chosen randomly. We will be calling out the winning numbers at the end of the competition. The trip will last four weeks, including the training that the kids will have to undergo before going up into space. Those who win will also be participants of an ISS study on the effects of developing bodies while in space." He turned to the camera. "So, all you kids between the ages of eleven and thirteen, go out there and start buying Tang for a chance to win. Good luck!"

Chapter 6

After the conference, Galen felt relaxed. It went better than he expected, though he still wished more reporters showed up. That was fine, John was right. More would show up when it came time for them to choose the winners. The reception they received from those who were there today was phenomenal. They all thought this was an amazing idea and the children would love it.

Galen went home that night and was able to finally have a good night's sleep. Since announcing his idea to the executives, he had restless nights always imagining the worst outcome. Now that one hurdle was out of the way, he was relieved. Tomorrow, the new products of Tang were being shipped to stores all across the world with the codes. The idea to make everything random was so that anyone, no matter where the children came from, was given the same fair chance to win.

Lost in his slumber, Galen's phone started to ring and vibrate across his nightstand. *What in the world,* he rubbed his eyes and took a few seconds to collect himself before he realized it was his phone. *Who would be calling me at this time?* He looked to his left, relieved to see that the phone didn't wake his wife. Hurriedly, he grabbed his phone and saw John's name on the screen. *Is he kidding me?*

"John, are you crazy calling me at this time? It's three in the morning!" He wasn't one to take such a tone with his boss, but he was finally having the sleep he deserved and hated being awakened at the early hours.

"Galen, I know this wasn't the best time to call, but I couldn't wait to tell you the news."

"What news?" Galen yawned.

"It's gone viral."

What is he talking about? Galen tried to concentrate on his phone. *Why can't he just cut to the chase?* "John, what's gone viral?"

"The press conference from yesterday. Turn on your television! You have to see this! All the major networks from across the country are playing it now."

Before Galen could respond, John hung up. He didn't want to get out of bed, but with the news he just heard, he couldn't pass this up. Putting his phone down, he got out of bed, careful not to wake his wife, and made his way downstairs to watch the news. He sat down on the couch and rubbed his eyes once again, making his vision clearer. Galen picked up the remote and turned on voice command. "Turn on Channel 338."

Nothing. *That's odd.* He checked the remote to make sure it was working but didn't find any problems. "Turn on Channel 338," he repeated. After a few seconds, the console in his living room opened up and a flat-screen raised up. *About time.* "Again. Turn on Channel 338," he said a final time, and static came across the screen as it turned on.

Galen waited for the news to come on, but instead, he

heard the AI voice coming over the speakers. "Galen? Are you asking for the television to be turned on now?"

Obviously, I'm trying to turn the television on, he rolled his eyes. "Yes, I need you to put on Channel 338 and hurry." Too much time was already wasted trying to get the television turned on and he didn't want to wait a second more.

"Galen," the voice spoke. "Are you aware it's three in the morning? Watching television now might wake your family."

"Yes, I'm aware that it's early in the morning. Please, just turn the channel on. He tried keeping his tone calm.

"But Galen, you never watch television this early in the morning. Are you sure this can't wait?"

If I could wait to watch the news, I wouldn't be awake now trying to get it on, he was getting annoyed. "Please, I'm not in the mood for a chat. I just want this channel on."

"I'm aware that you keep asking me to turn the television on, but I'm just making sure you realize the hour and how you're not on your schedule."

"I really do miss the days when I didn't have to talk to inanimate objects to get them to turn on," he muttered. "At least, back then, I could turn electronics on whenever I wanted to and not rely on the AI to do the job."

"I heard that, Galen," the AI said. "As you requested,

here is Channel 338," and she went quiet.

Finally, Galen wanted to scream as Channel 338 came up on the screen. The first news story was shown in English for the kids in America. Galen laughed, wondering who in America was awake at this time. *I guess it's possible some might be crazy like I am right now, awake and watching the news.*

The second story on the screen was directed towards those living in India, dubbed in their language. Clips were added in of children waiting outside stores to purchase as many cans of Tang as they could. Things weren't much different in the news story that came from Great Britain as children waited outside the stores for their chance to purchase winning cans. It amazed Galen that these kids and their parents were willing to wait outside for hours. In Japan, the anchor told the children what they had to do in order to win the contest before going back to the main news program.

"Turn TV off," Galen said and went back upstairs, in shock that in such a short amount of time the conference went viral. This was exactly what he needed to be assured that his idea for the contest would be a successful one. When he returned to bed, he was too excited to sleep and laid in bed looking up at the ceiling. Tomorrow was going to be a great day.

Chapter 7

No sleep came to Galen that night, and how could it? When John called him early in the morning, he thought he was exaggerating about the conference going viral. Now, he knew that was true. He was still in shock at the fact of how many countries saw him on television announcing the contest.

His alarm went off a few hours after he returned to bed. He got ready for work and headed to headquarters greeted by John when he walked through the doors.

"How amazing was that coverage we got for the contest?" John asked.

"Honestly, I thought you were just saying that to make me feel better about the contest. But when I saw the news, I couldn't believe it. Our conference reached all the way to Japan!"

"I think it's safe to say that this contest is going to be a hit. Come, we have the follow-up conference today," John directed him to the conference room.

"Please tell me there are more people here today than there were yesterday," Galen worried.

"Why don't you see for yourself," John smiled as he opened the door.

Galen couldn't believe his eyes. Yesterday, you could see

the empty seats. Today, you couldn't see any empty spaces, if there were any. At least seventy reporters were waiting for John and Galen to speak. John pulled Galen aside. "Galen, sales are going to go through the roof. We need to hire more people. Call HR and tell them to do whatever they can to hire. We're going to need more employees."

Galen nodded and rushed off to his office. He knew it was only a matter of time before he and John would have to meet up to discuss everything with the reporters. He knew it was going to be crazy at work today, but he didn't know it was going to be this crazy. John was right, they were going to need more people on board to work for Tang in order to keep up with the sales.

*****

All across the world, people were rushing out to buy Tang for their children, each and every one of them hoping they had a winning can. People were climbing over one another reaching for as many cans as they could carry. One would think it was Black Friday the way fights were breaking out over Tang. Galen watched some of the coverage in his office and chuckled at the scenes. *I didn't expect people would get agitated over getting cans of Tang,* he laughed. It was safe to say, the contest would definitely raise sales.

While people were going crazy across the globe, it was hysteria downstairs in the lobby of Tang Headquarters. Phones were ringing off the hook, Caden, the lobby attendant, couldn't handle them on his own. "Please hold." "Please hold." "Please hold." He answered every phone call transferring them to Galen's phone.

"Excuse me!" A wealthy woman and her tween son walked up to Caden's desk. He was busy on the phone transferring more calls and didn't hear the woman until she raised her voice. "I said excuse me!"

Caden jumped at the sound of her voice. "I'm sorry, it's kind of busy here today. How may I help you," he asked trying to answer calls at the same time.

"I would like to buy a truckload of Tang. I want my son to win this contest and he always gets what he wants. She pulled her checkbook out. "Name the price, I'll pay anything."

"Sorry, but that's impossible. We won't sell a truckload of Tang to one customer. We want it to be fair to everyone who wants to enter. You'll have to do what everyone else is doing, go to your local store to purchase the cans," Caden explained.

"I don't understand, I'm offering to pay for the Tang. Cash? Is it cash you want?" the woman begged.

"What I want is for you to please leave. I can't bend the rules for you because you want your son to win," he pointed towards the door. "As you can see, I need to tend to these phone calls. Please leave."

*****

Later that morning, Galen joined John with the other executives as they prepared for the press conference. They sat in the room watching the sales go up every second. "Galen, what can I say? You were right," John shook his hand. "The sales are out of this world. I don't think Tang ever saw them this high, not even when they first started."

Galen nodded watching a video on his laptop. "Guys, you need to see this. There's chaos all over the world with people pushing their way into stores. Bet the workers never thought they'd see the day when customers would be fighting for Tang," he laughed.

The executives gathered around Galen's laptop to watch the footage when Hannah, Galen's secretary, walked into the room. "John. Galen. The press is ready for the conference."

John and Galen walked into the press room, a look of amazement on their faces. Since they last checked the room, more reporters piled in. There wasn't room for anyone else to attend today's conference. "Let's do this," John said.

John and Galen welcomed the press and immediately hands were in the air. John looked at Galen and nodded, giving him the go-ahead to get everything started. After all, this was all his idea, he should be the one to speak about it.

"I want to thank you for coming today. I'm sure you've all seen our conference from yesterday explaining the contest, so today we are here to take any questions you might have.

Majority of the questions were about how Galen came up with the idea for the contest which he answered about the conversation he had with his son that one night. He was getting bored of all the same questions until one reporter raised his hand and asked, "What do you hope will come out of this contest?"

"That's an interesting question," Galen said. "I'm hoping, not only will it bring attention to Tang, but I'm also hoping that it will open up people to learn more about the ISS. We're going to have six tweens going up into space. With this, we could be opening space exploration to millions of others. And we can look back and say, we helped."

He looked at the time and noticed it was getting late. "Thank you, everyone, for coming. Unfortunately, that's all the time we have today for questions. We will have another conference closer to the end of the contest."

Chapter 8

Brandon set his alarm extra early this morning, wanting to be one of the first people at the local convenience store. Since seeing the news conference, he knew he was going to buy as many cans as he could to make sure he won a trip to the ISS. That would be a dream come true for him. How could he not win this trip of a lifetime?

His parents already left for work, leaving him on his own to get to the store. He woke up at five in the morning, giving him more than enough time to get ready for the day. Once he was ready, he went over to his desk and grabbed the rocket-shaped bank. *I wonder how much I have in here. Hope it's enough.* It had been a while since he last put some money in the bank, but it couldn't be empty. He hadn't taken any money out of it since he bought some space magazines. He shook it and a frown appeared across his face when nothing came out. *That's odd. Maybe I did spend it all.*

Brandon wasn't going to give up. There had to be money in his room. Then he remembered his hiding spot inside his closet. He rushed over and pushed his clothes aside, revealing the fake platform that opened up. He smiled when he saw a few dollars. It wasn't much, but it would have to do. If he wanted to buy more Tang, he would have to ask his parents for some money when they came home, but he couldn't wait until then.

The sun was shining as he left his house and walked over to his bike. *This has to be a sign that good things are to come my way.* He didn't waste another second in heading to the convenience store, *Casey's Market & Deli*.

Brandon arrived at *Casey's Market & Deli* and was surprised when he didn't see a line outside. It was only five minutes after seven and he hated being even a few minutes late. Seeing no kids around his age outside calmed him down. *Casey's Market & Deli* wasn't known as a popular store in town. Everyone else probably went to the well-known ones while he came here. He shrugged as he got off his bike and walked into the store, hoping he would come out with a few cans of Tang.

Once inside the store, Brandon made his way to the juice aisle and stopped short when he didn't see any cans of Tang. *That's odd...I bet they have it behind the counter so they could keep count on how many were sold*, he tried to keep his spirits up. He walked over to an employee at the front register. "Excuse me, I was hoping you could help me."

"Let me guess, you're here to buy some Tang," the employee said.

"Yes," Brandon smiled. "I didn't see any on the shelf. Do you have any back here?"

"Sorry kid, someone else around your age bought us out a couple of minutes ago. He was here waiting for us at seven in the morning."

"Do you have any in the back or something?"

The employee shook his head.
"I'm sorry, we couldn't say no, not when he had the

money to buy them all. Maybe you should go check out the other stores in town. They might have some left."

Brandon nodded, defeated. He didn't know what else to do. Even if he were to go to the other stores in town, by the time he arrived, they would be sold out as well. He thanked the employee one last time before sadly walking out of the store. He couldn't give up. There had to be a can of Tang somewhere that was meant for him to buy.

*****

In Lyon, France, a mother and daughter were riding their bikes through the countryside, enjoying the nice weather. But the girl's mind was elsewhere.

The girl smiled as she reached the convenience store with her mother. She walked up to a large stack of Tang containers. She looked at the containers before finally settling on one. "Celui-la." ("This one.") The mother nodded and smiled. Both of them walked up to the front counter.

"Quelqu'un veut aller dans l'espace." ("Someone wants to go into space") said the clerk.

"Oui" ("Yes") she responded in excitement. She handed the money to pay.

The clerk leaned over and gave her the change. "Bonne chance." ("Good luck.")

"Merci!" ("Thank You") The girl skipped out of the store with the bag in her hand and her mother following close behind.

40

Chapter 9

Brandon refused to give up. Not every store in town could be sold out of Tang. One store, that's all he needed, to have even one can of Tang for him to purchase. He rode his bike through the streets, a frown on his face when he saw signs on the windows stating they were out of Tang. *Is there any store in town that hasn't sold out?*

Still, quitting wasn't an option. There was still one store left that he hadn't checked. *The Village Crossing* was a small convenience shop on the other side of town. It wasn't a place he normally traveled alone, but he had no other choice. This shop was his last hope.

He reached the store and parked his bike to find Ethan leaving the store with his mother. In his hand was a bag full of cans of Tang while his mother held two bags with the same contents.

"Oh, great," sighed Brandon upon seeing Ethan leaving the store.

Brandon walked into the store where he saw a sign at the entrance: **BUY TANG FOR YOUR CHANCE TO WIN A TRIP TO THE INTERNATIONAL SPACE STATION.**

Brandon's heart skipped a beat. There was a crowd of people gathered around one employee, waving money in their hands all asking to purchase as many cans of Tang they could afford. Brandon reached into his pocket and took out three dollar bills, the only money he could find in his room.

If I didn't spend so much on all my space books and magazines, I would be able to afford more Tang. He didn't know how much it was for one can, but he hoped he could buy at least one.

He looked to find an employee who wasn't busy with a crowd when he saw an older gentleman behind the counter. "Excuse me," he walked up to the counter. "I was wondering if you would be able to help me."

The older clerk looked up at him from his magazine. "Let me guess, you're one of the kids who's looking for a can of Tang. That's all I've seen coming in here today. Kid after kid wanting to buy Tang because of this contest."

"Well, I..." Brandon looked out the window and saw Ethan and his mother packing their trunk with the bags of Tang they bought. "I was. But I doubt there's any left by now," he sighed. "I guess once again I'm too late," he said as he began to leave the store.

"Wait a second," the clerk called him over.

"Yes?" Brandon walked back.

"I thought I recognized you. Aren't you the kid who won the Appleton Science Fair? I saw you on the news."

"Yeah, that's me," Brandon smiled.

The clerk smiled. "Did you know, I also won the Appleton Science Fair back in 1978."

"Really?" Brandon was amazed.
"Yes, really. Come to think of it, my project was a rocket too. Though, it wasn't as advanced as yours was and it didn't send a satellite into space. I wanted to become an astronaut more than anything."

"I want to be an astronaut too!" Brandon exclaimed.

The clerk smiled and said, "Though I never made it to outer space, I never gave up on the dream. Although, at my age, I'm too old to go to space now. Listen, you invested your money in helping people. That in my book is more important than anything else." He reached down and grabbed a can of Tang, handing it over to Brandon. "I'm too old for this contest, but you seem to be the right age. Here you go."

"Thank you!" Brandon reached into his pocket for his money but the clerk stopped him.

"Don't worry about it. This is on me," he smiled.

"I..I can't thank you enough for this. But, thank you."

"I understand tomorrow is the big day. They're going to announce the winners."

"Yes. I'm nervous. I hope this is the winning can."

"Well, the best of luck to you," the clerk said.

Brandon thanked him again before heading out of the store with a better feeling than what he had when he walked in. He couldn't explain the feeling he had, but something told him that this was a lucky can. All there was left to do was make it through the day and wait for the winners to be announced.

He retrieved his bike and happily rode home. He couldn't wait for his parents to return from work so he could tell them the great news. The second he got through the door, he placed the can on the shelf in his bedroom for safe keeping. He could hardly contain his excitement each time he looked at it. Perhaps this container held the answer to making his dream come true.

Chapter 10

Today was the day children across the world were waiting for, the winners of the Tang contest were going to be announced. Across the globe, children sat in front of their televisions all day watching the news. With the matter of one contest, Tang managed to grab the attention of every child in the world.

John and Galen were in the conference room at Tang Headquarters surrounded by reporters. Over two hundred showed up, crammed into the room. Never before had they seen so many reporters for their company and Galen was beginning to wonder if they should've moved the conference to an auditorium. It was too late now. They were going live in a matter of a few minutes to read the winning codes. First, they were going to answer questions.

"John, we've estimated over 2.3 billion people are watching today's conference. What is going through your mind at this moment?" a reporter asked.

"When you put it that way, the first thing on my mind is, what are the other seven billion people doing right now if they aren't watching us?" John laughed and the others in the room joined.

"There are more people watching this than last year's Super Bowl. That is something all of us here at Tang are happy about. Who knew a simple drink contest would outdo the Super Bowl," Galen added. He turned to John. "What do you say, shall we start announcing the winning codes?"

"I think we made the kids wait long enough," John smiled. "Here we go. The code for the first winner is," he pulled a piece of paper out of the box. "894GH31423."

*****

The smile on Brandon's face disappeared as he sat in his living room and looked at his lid. "Not even close," he sighed looking at his parents.

"Don't worry about it, son," his father patted him on the back. "That was only the first code. There are still five more they need to announce."

*****

In Japan, a girl turns to her father with a huge smile on her face, handing him her lid. "Watashi wa watashi ga katta to!" ("I think I won!")

The father took a look at the lid before double checking it with the live feed he was watching on his laptop. He turned to his wife, his face widened with a smile. "Watashitachi no musume wa uchu suteshon ni ikimasu." ("Our daughter is going to the space station.")

*****

John reached into the box to pick out the second winner. "Alright, we have winner number two. 79AT19346."

*****

Brandon stared blankly at the television. Sensing he was upset, his mother sat beside him on the couch and put her arm around him. "Don't give up, Brandon. There are still four more winners to be called."

"I know," he nodded and forced a weak smile. He didn't want to show his parents that he was about to give up thinking he could win this contest.

*****

A group of boys gathered around a computer in Calcutta, India with Tang lids across the table. The second John announced the second code, they all looked at their lids. One boy looked over at another's lid and smiled. "Mukesh! You won! You have a winning lid!"

"I....I did?" Mukesh was in shock.

"Yes!" the boys stood up and cheered. One of his friends got up and ran outside and yelled, "MUKESH WON!!! HE'S GOING TO THE SPACE STATION!!"

*****

John waited a few minutes as he did after announcing each winner before getting to the next one, giving children a chance to see if they won. "Alright, we have a third winner chosen. The code is 2836LC9918."

*****

Brandon sighed and continued to hope. With three more winners to come, he tried to reassure himself that he still had a chance to win.

*****

In Nairobi, Kenya, a group of tween girls sat around a television listening to the winners being announced. One of the girls stood up and walked outside, holding onto a lid. Her friends followed her. "Nadhani Amondi alishinda." ("I think Amondi won!")

They followed their friend outside where she took the lid and held it up to the sky.

*****

"Everyone, we're getting close to the end. So here is the fourth winner," John continued. "Look under your lids to see if you have the code," he turned to Galen. "Since this was your idea, why don't you read out the numbers now."

Galen nodded and took the paper from John's hand. "Code 636JN35522."

*****

In Brazil, a boy sat in front of his television, reading his lid carefully after Galen announced the code. "Eu venci" ("I WON!") he jumped up and down. "Eu venci" ("I WON!")

His father walked over and double-checked the lid. He smiled at his son and patted him on the back.

*****

Brandon looked dejected. "Didn't win. I think I'll go to bed," he frowned.

His father looked over at him, "Don't give up, Brandon. There are still two more winners. You never know what will

50

happen."

Brandon wanted to believe his father, but he was losing all hope. *Alright, I'll stay until all the winners are announced, but I doubt any of them will be me.*

*****

Galen continued to choose the winners. "Fifth code five goes to, 1916KS3512."

*****

Meanwhile in Lyon, France the French girl who went out earlier with her mother to buy the container of Tang sat in front of the computer watching the drawing. The second Galen said the last number to the code, she looked at her mother with a huge smile on her face.

*****

Brandon walked out of the living room, not saying a word. His parents knew this was another code he didn't win, but they didn't want to give up hope. There was still one last winner left to be announced and they hoped it belonged to their son. After getting a cup of water to calm himself down, Brandon returned back to the living room when Galen was about to announce the last winner.

Brandon picked up his lid and began to mouth out the numbers and letters that belonged to his code. After realizing he was saying exactly the same thing Galen was announcing on television, he realized he had a winning lid. He turned to his parents with a smile. "I won! I won!"

His parents got up off their chairs and hugged their son. "Brandon, do you realize what this means? Your dream is coming true and you'll be going up into space," his father said.

Even knowing he was one of the few winners, Brandon was in shock that he was being given the chance to go up into space. This wasn't an opportunity many experienced. He was one of the lucky few.

Chapter 11

There were mixed emotions going on around the world after all the winners were announced for the Tang contest. So many children rushed out to buy cans of Tang, all hoping for the same outcome, that they would be winners. There was no doubt there would be upset children. But no one could be as upset as Ethan, who was sure he was going to win a trip to the ISS.

"THIS ISN'T FAIR!" Ethan yelled from a sitting position on the floor in his living room, surrounded by Tang lids. "This isn't fair! I must've misread one of the codes on these lids. One of them has to be a winner. How could I not win with all the Tang we bought?!" he demanded.

"Ethan, I checked all the lids yesterday and double checked this morning. None of them are the codes he announced," his mother tried to soothe him, but he didn't want to hear it.

"THIS CONTEST WAS RIGGED!" Ethan stormed to his room and slammed the door.

*****

A few days later, once everything was set up with all the winners in connection with NASA, the calls went out. Colin Sandberg, the person in charge of training at Strato-Labs and NASA was put in charge of all the calls. One by one, he called all across the world; Japan, India, France, Kenya, Brazil, and in his own homeland, America, to speak to the parents of the children and explain their preparation before they would be going into space for the study.

Training would last three weeks starting on the 28th of the month where the children would arrive in Houston with their parents. When the phone calls were finished, Culin went back to work making sure everything was going according to plan with Strato-Labs. Everyone knew they were taking a risk having kids go up into space, something that was never done before, for a study. As long as all the kids passed the training tests, they shouldn't encounter any problems. They would be on board the ISS with astronauts who would be nearby to help in any way.

*****

Ethan stepped outside to his front lawn and set up a table. In front of it, he hung a sign: **TANG CANS 50 CENTS.** Once he had the cans set up on the table, he took a seat behind it.

"TANG! GET YOUR CANS OF TANG HERE! ONLY 50 CENTS!"

*****

The following Friday, Galen and a woman sat at the Houston Airport. In the woman's hand was a notepad screen with the kids' names listed on it that she would check off as they arrived. One by one their flights landed and were greeted by Galen and the woman.

A Japanese girl walked up to the woman with her father and looked at the screen. "That's me," she smiled pointing to the name Sumie.

The woman crossed off Sumie's name and smiled. "Welcome, Sumie! I'm Sharon Dellamonte from Strato-Labs and this is Galen Noble from Tang. Please be seated over there with the rest of the winners. We're just waiting for everyone to arrive."

"There's only one more person we're waiting for and then we can be on our way," Galen added.

Sumie nodded and walked over to the seats where she saw a Brazilian boy talking to a French girl.

Bored with the French girl, who wasn't showing the boy any attention, he then turned around and smiled at Sumie. "You from Japan?" he went over to her family. "Wonder if you can bring sushi onto the rocket. I loved sushi.

"I doubt we'll be able to have sushi while in space," Sumie said before the boy's attention was distracted.

"Look! A dog!" he pointed out as an Indian man and boy with a service dog approached Sharon and Galen.

"Hi," the father introduced himself to Sharon and Galen. This is my son, Mukesh," he pointed to the young boy wearing sunglasses.

"Your name is Mukesh Sanjay?" Sharon asked the boy.

"That's me," the boy smiled. "I won the Tang Spaceflight contest. And this is my dog, Sumit. His name means 'good friend' in Hindi."

Sharon glanced at Galen waiting for him to respond. He leaned down to the boy's level. "It's a pleasure to meet you, Mukesh. Please have a seat with the other winners and their families. We'll be leaving shortly."

Mukesh's family joined the group of winners when the Brazilian boy went up to Sumit who started to chase him in a circle. "AHHH! HELP! I'M GETTING TANGLED IN HIS LEASH!" he laughed as the dog continued to chase him around.

Galen and Sharon walked away from the winners while they took a conference phone call. "What am I supposed to do?" Galen said, while on the phone. "No, we didn't have it in fine print. How could we? Do you have any idea how horrible it would've sounded if we said no one with disabilities can enter the contest? Anyways, I don't see it being a problem if he passes the physical tests."

"Don't forget, he has a service dog," Sharon added.

"Will they allow the dog?" Galen asked.

"A dog has been sent to space before. I don't think we'll have a problem with them allowing Mukesh's dog going along with him."

The phone call ended and the two looked at each other with a worried and uncertain expression. "I'll call Strato-Labs and let them know that we'll need dog food waiting for us when we arrive. And everything else they would think one would need for a dog at the training center," Galen said.

After the phone call was made to Strato-Labs, Galen and

Sharon walked over to the group of winners and their parents. "Great news. I just got off the phone with Strato-Labs and they're ready for our arrival. The cars are waiting outside, please follow me," Galen said.

The group arrived at Strato-Labs where Sharon took over bringing them to their lodging section. "This is where you're staying tonight and where your families will be living for the next three weeks as you train for the spaceflight. Inside your rooms, you will find your welcome packet which has an emergency number if you need help at any point during the night. Every room has face recognition to allow all of you into any of the accessible rooms. Those rooms are listed so you know which ones are prohibited to the contest winners and their families. Tomorrow will be an 8 o'clock wake-up call for breakfast and then it's off to training. Now, get some sleep. You're going to need it," she smiled before leaving the families on their own.

*****

In the middle of the night, Rafi opened the door from his room and stepped out into the hall. Nothing but darkness in the hallway. He was bored in the room and couldn't sleep due to the excitement of what waited for him tomorrow during training. He found the training module hangar and walked in. Reaching across the wall, he hoped to find a light switch but instead turned on the alarms. *What do I do now? I'm not supposed to be in here,* he froze as the alarm blared and the lights flickered.

Seconds later, he was being escorted back to his room by a night guard. The guard knocked on his door. "Is this your son?" the guard asked when Rafi's father opened the door in his pajamas.

He looked down and saw his son with a small smile on his face. "Yes, he's my son. Is he in trouble?"

The guard shook his head. "I understand he might be excited to be here so I'll put in the official report that he was sleepwalking. Please, make sure he stays in his room for the rest of the night."

Rafi's father thanked the guard and closed the door, making sure Rafi went straight to bed. Tomorrow would be arriving soon.

Chapter 12

Morning came early and the winners were awake with excitement when they got their wake-up call. Once breakfast was finished, it was time to get down to business starting with a press conference.

"Everyone, if you'll follow me," Sharon directed the winners and their families out of the dining room and down the hall. "We are going to enter the training hangar where you will be greeted by reporters. I don't want any of you to be nervous. She opened the door, allowing the kids to walk in first, all of them wearing space jumpsuits sporting Tang and Strato-Labs' logos.

"WOW!" the kids all said in unison except for Rafi who smirked, knowing his secret of visiting this room last night. *This looks familiar.*

Once the kids were lined up in front of the hangar, reporters from all over the world began to take their pictures. Sharon walked over to the group and turned on the television screen showing three American astronauts and three Russian cosmonauts floating across the screen. Sharon took a spot next to Galen at the podium to officially welcome the winners.

"Good morning," she smiled at the children. "This is the ISS Training Hangar where you'll be spending the next three weeks as we prepare you for your historic journey to the ISS. First, we want to introduce you to the world. Please take a seat at the table where your nameplates are situated and

Galen will say a few words," she stepped aside.

Galen waited for the kids to be settled in their seats before taking over. "Good morning everyone and welcome to Strato-Labs Training facility here in Houston. Seated before all of you are the six winners of the joint contest Tang had with Strato-Labs." He then turned to the kids. "Could you all, one at a time, tell everyone your name and what country you're from?"

Sumie started the introductions. "I'm Sumie and I'm from Japan."

"I'm Brandon and I'm representing America."

"My name is Genevieve and I'm from France."

"Name is Rafi and I'm from Brazil!" He looked around the table in front of him. "And I do magic...Has anyone seen my playing cards?"

Brandon raised his hand and smiled, "I made them disappear." Some of the reporters chuckled at Brandon's joke.

"I'm Mukesh and this is my dog Sumit. I'm from India."

"Amondi and I'm from Kenya," she ended the introductions before Galen returned to the microphone.

"At this time, we will welcome any questions, either to us or the children."

"Are you concerned that you're sending these inexperienced kids up into space without any adults?" journalist, Rick Soto, asked the first question.

"I can answer that one," Sharon said. "They will be going up into space on the Star-Reacher 1000, the newest of our rockets. Everything is controlled from the launch room. With the self-launching technology powered and controlled by eight satellites, the kids won't have to worry about taking control of anything while in the rocket. And thanks to the new air-blaster rocket, designed by MENLO Ride, the kids will be meeting the astronauts aboard the ISS within thirty minutes. We plan on breaking the record with this launch and the kids won't be on their own for long."

Sharon looked out at the reporters and asked, "Any other questions?" Rafi raised his hand. Sharon smiled and said, "Yes, Rafi?"

"Yeah, I'm still looking for my cards...have you seen them?'

Some of the reporters laughed again. Genevieve turned and looked at Rafi. "How are you going to keep the playing cards in place with zero gravity?"

Rafi scratched his head and replied, "Hmm, never thought about that."

They took a few more questions from the reporters, mostly asking the kids how excited they were to be the first kids into space. Pressed for time, Sharon had to cut the questions off.

"Let me direct you all to a live video feed that is coming in from those currently aboard the ISS. She turned to the screen where everyone saw the astronauts and cosmonauts floating around the ISS.

"Greetings from the International Space Station. I'm Commander Brian Vacarr and on behalf of myself and all the astronauts and cosmonauts here, we are looking forward to meeting all the winners." He stopped and looked back when he heard an alarm going off behind him. "What's that?" he asked quietly.

"Nothing," a cosmonaut said pressing a button. "All fixed."

Brian turned back to the screen. "That's nothing to worry about. I believe that was the alarm for one of our two external cooling loops. Cosmonaut Nebikov is taking care of it. How about if I ask you the contestants a question. Does anyone know how the ISS is cooled?"

Brandon was the first to raise his hand. "Ammonia circulated outside the station through giant radiators to keep it cool," he smiled.

"Correct. I couldn't have said it better myself," Brian smiled. He turned when Cosmonaut Nebikov noted that the situation was taken care of. "See, what did I say? A simple fix. Nothing to worry about. The ISS is like a gently-used eighteen-year-old car. Sometimes it requires a little maintenance. I have to go now, but we'll see you soon."

"That's all the time we have for now," Sharon said to the reporters. "It's time we get these kids started with their training. Three weeks from today the Strato-Labs launch will take place and we hope to see all of you there." She turned to the children. "Please follow me. The first stop is the weightless chamber."

Excited, the children stepped into the weightless chamber, laughing as they floated around the room, bumping into each other. Brandon and Amondi started a game of weightless tag. Floating close by was Sumit, the dog.

"Wait!" Sharon watched from the control room and couldn't find Rafi on the monitor. "Where did Rafi go? Didn't he go inside..." she stopped and shook her head when she saw Rafi's face poke out of the dog cage. Out of the winners, he was the one she would have to keep an eye on.

*****

Chapter 13

Before they knew it, launch day had arrived, but not without problems along the way, starting with the kids getting dressed in their spacesuits. Everyone was dressed and ready for their final physicals before getting ready for the launch when they heard a girl scream and stomp her feet.

"It's orange!" Genevieve cried. "The spacesuit has orange on it! I can't be seen in orange!"

"Why not? It's only two orange stripes," Rafi teased.

I hate the color orange. It doesn't compliment my complexion. I wear colors like pink and purple. Couldn't they give us a choice as to what color spacesuit we would want? And now people are going to see me on television wearing this. I'll be made fun of back home for this."

Sharon and Galen walked into the room to gather the winners, ignoring Genevieve's complaints.

"Okay, everyone!," Sharon got their attention. "If you follow us, we're going to take you to the launch pad. There are reporters outside the hangar waiting. You don't have to say anything to them, just smile and wave."

The winners exited the hangar, waving to the reporters as they followed Sharon and Galen. Drones flew around taking video and pictures for the world to see this historical moment. The kids ran over to hug their parents one last time before leaving.

"Everyone, we really need to leave if we want to make it on time," Galen said from a self-driving van. A final goodbye, the kids followed and entered the van, looks of excitement on their faces.

Minutes later, the kids arrived at the launch pad and were greeted by a Strato-Labs employee. "Welcome. This way please."

The kids looked around at one another, their expressions changed. This was really happening, they were going to be the first kids in space. There was no backing out as they entered the rocket. Next stop, the ISS with only thirty-two minutes and sixteen seconds left until blastoff.

Once they were all inside, it was time for a final vitals testing. "This is an easy test," the voice of the launch command controller came across the speakers. "All you need to do is blink as responses. First, I need to test your ocu-vital lenses. Blink twice." The kids blinked in unison. "Great. And from what I see, you're all strapped in and so is the dog in his cage."

*****

"Liftoff will be happening in 5...4...3...2...1. LIFTOFF!"

In the stands, sat their parents and media watching as these six children made history. Cheers could be heard for miles as the rocket lifted off into space. This was a day that many across the globe would remember forever.

"This is Star-Reacher Command," a voice came over the speaker. Blink twice." Each of the contestants blinked twice to show that they understood what was being said. "Perfect. Now, why don't you tell me how the voyage is going so far?"

The kids all looked at each other, neither one knowing who should speak first until Rafi smiled and opened his mouth. "I have to fart!"

"You do know you don't have to hold it in," command laughed over the speaker.

"I know, but I want to wait until I'm in outer space to see what happens when I fart," Rafi laughed.

"There's no need to wait. It's been done before and nothing happened. All a myth that something amazing happens when you fart in outer space," command laughed. "If I were you, I wouldn't wait."

There wasn't another response from Rafi, but the smile on his face showed he felt relieved. "You were right, it was better I let that out." Everyone laughed, including command, at his statement.

"I have a report," command said. "You are officially astronauts as you've just reached outer space. You've done something that no child has ever done before. Congratulations."

"WOOHOO!! NEXT STOP...INTERNATIONAL SPACE STATION!" Mukesh couldn't contain his excitement.

"That's right, Mukesh. The crew is waiting for your arrival," command pointed out.

"Hey! Tell them not to use the bathroom when we get there because I really have to go!" Rafi exclaimed.

"I'm almost afraid to see what's going to happen when he takes the spacesuit off," Brandon whispered to Genevieve. She shook her head at the thought.

"What is it with boys and farts. It's gross if you ask me," as she made a face.

The kids continued to talk about their excitement when command came over the speakers one last time. "You will be docking at ISS in three minutes. I repeat, you will be docking in three minutes."

Chapter 14

Three minutes later, the rocket came to a stop and the kids couldn't contain the happiness they felt. They finally made it. They were finally in outer space. They waited for the hatch to open inside the ISS. For the six of them, this was a dream come true. Standing before them were the astronauts and cosmonauts waiting to greet them.

"We've been waiting for your arrival," one of the men said. "I'm Commander Shelton, but you can call me Cal. Welcome to the ISS. You can all unbuckle now."

One by one, the kids unbuckled and started to float around the ISS. "This is unbelievable!" Rafi announced. "Look what I can do! I can do some weird kind of breakdance. I need to bring this back home and do the same moves!"

Cal laughed as he watched Rafi trying to dance while he floated. "I'll let you all get adjusted and then I'll be moving you into the other room. We will start the testing soon."

Cal split the children up for testing in order for them not to be on top of one another. One group of kids was going off with one of the astronauts to test the geometry of cell and tissue growth on developing bodies while aboard the ISS while the other group went off to test cardio and blood circulation on kids in space. He walked over to Mukesh and put his hand on his shoulder. "I'm going to bring you and Sumit to a special room to make sure you're both doing well on this trip." He was glad that headquarters alerted him beforehand that a blind child would be on the I.S.S. This would be a great way to test people with disabilities and their travel into space.

He brought Mukesh and Sumit to a workout area equipped with exercise gear. "I want to make sure your vitals haven't changed. This is called the Colbert Treadmill, a specially-designed treadmill that allows people to run while on the I.S.S." He helped guide Mukesh on the machine. There was enough room for Sumit to be alongside his master. "Don't worry, I'm here keeping an eye on you both," Cal smiled as he took notes on Mukesh and Sumit.

While everyone was busy with the contestants, they didn't know that another problem was arising in the space station. An astronaut contacted Star-Reach command. "How can we help you?"

"Hey, It's Commander Vacarr here. We need more coolant valves and please include it with critical cargo on the next ISS mission. Until then, we're lowering the cooling system by twenty percent. I don't want to worry you, but I think it's necessary."

"Copy," command center responded.

*****

Those at command didn't want to alarm the kids about the report from the astronaut and for the rest of the day, they acted as if there was nothing to worry about. Cal knew better, if this wasn't taken care of soon, they could all be in danger. Everyone retired for the night and he checked on the kids in their sleeping quarters before heading back to the astronaut sleeping quarters.

"Hey!" Rafi floated across the room with his eyes closed. "Look at me, I'm sleep floating. Get it? Not sleepwalking, but sleep floating," he joked. The others began to laugh.

As he floated in his sleep, he had a hand out of his sleeping bag, and accidentally hit an alarm.

"IS EVERYONE ALRIGHT?" Cal floated into their room, startling all the kids. He pressed a few buttons and the alarms went silent.

'I..I'm sorry," Rafi's lips quivered. "I must've hit it by accident."

"Maybe you shouldn't be clowning around while we're here," Brandon muttered under his breath.

"Everything is fine," Cal quickly said. "You didn't do anything wrong. We are aware of this problem already. Just try to get some sleep," continued Cal before leaving the room.

It didn't take long after the excitement for the children to fall back asleep. The trip to the ISS tired them out. Suddenly, the equipment in the room shutdown.

"What was that?" Amondi asked as she looked around.

"I don't know," replied Brandon. He looked around the room to see the emergency lights on. *This can't be good*. He got out of his sleeping bag and Rafi joined him going in different directions. Rafi floated to the glass door separating them from the astronauts while Brandon went to the control panel and began to hit the switches. *Something here has got to turn the equipment back on.*

"Brandon, what's going on?" Rafi asked, putting their differences aside.

"Nothing is working. What about you?"

Rafi shook his head. "I can't get the door to open."

*****

Chaos occupied Launch Command as the alarms went crazy. The night supervisor rushed over to the control panel and began to push the buttons with the help of his skeleton crew, but nothing worked. The alarms continued to grow louder and it was then, Launch Command knew they were in trouble. They needed help and quick. The night supervisor rushed to the video phone and called ISS Chief Director, Lestor Jacobs.

"Hello?" Lester rubbed the sleep out of his eyes as he sat up in his bed.

"We have a serious situation going on with the ISS right now. And we need help. The alarms won't go off and we can't tell what is causing the problem. What do we do?" the supervisor panicked.

*****

The astronauts and cosmonauts stared helplessly through the glass door at the children. Cal tried to pry open the door so they could be with the children, knowing they must be afraid, but no matter what he tried, the door wouldn't budge.

"What do you think happened?" Brian asked.

"I think the cooling system overheated, causing the power outage," Cal tried his best to calculate the situation.

"What about the emergency generator? It should've kicked on by now. Why hasn't it? Doesn't it also regulate the oxygen levels too?" a cosmonaut asked.

Cal nodded. "We better figure out what to do and soon. Their parents are trusting us to keep their kids safe and protect them. How can we do that if we can't even be with them during an emergency?"

Chapter 15

It didn't take long before news about the incident on the ISS hit the public airwaves. In Times Square, a crowd gathered around the immense digital screen where a news anchor sat at her desk, ashen face waiting for the go-ahead to give her report.

"This is a special report. News Channel Five has just received a report that there is a situation aboard the ISS. That is all we have for now, but we will keep you updated as the news unfolds. I was told, however, to let everyone know there is no cause for an alarm. The children are with trained professionals who know what to do in times such as these. I will be back when more news comes in."

*****

Brandon's mother and father sat in front of their television, at the Space Center. Their son, their only child, who they allowed to go on this trip was now in danger. His father was silent as his mother cried. She felt responsible for signing the consent form knowing that there were many risk factors in letting her son go off into space with no experience.

All I want is for him to come back home, she looked up at the ceiling wondering what was going through her son's mind during this time.

*****

Aboard the ISS, the astronauts and cosmonauts were

trying to figure out what to do in this situation. The children looked at them helplessly through the glass door desperately wanting a way to communicate. "What are we supposed to do?" a cosmonaut broke the silence in their room. We can't contact Launch Command and as long as we can't get the door to open, we can't communicate with the kids."

"First, we remain calm," Commander Vacarr said. "We don't need to make the kids nervous or think we don't know what to do. Second, we go old school," he pointed to the door. "It's the only thing we can do to help them."

The rest of the astronauts and cosmonauts agreed. If they wanted to be able to help the kids get through this, they would have to remain calm to communicate with the children. The parents put their trust in them to take care of their kids and they would do whatever it took to keep them safe.

On the other side, the children were doing all that they could in order to call for help. Genevieve looked at Amondi who sat by the phones. "Any luck getting a hold of Launch Command using the backup phones?"

"I'm trying," Amondi frowned. "But nothing is working. The systems are down."

"This is all my fault,' Rafi looked down at his feet. "I hit the switch and then the alarm went off. None of this would've happened if I had just kept my hands to my sides." Sumit barked, causing Rafi to look in his direction.

"Sumit says that it's not your fault," Mukesh reassured

the boy. "And Sumit knows what he's talking about. You aren't responsible for this."

Rafi smiled, feeling a little less guilty. Didn't Cal say that they were aware of the situation? That means something else was going on long before he hit the switch.

*****

Those working at Launch Command were going crazy with the phone calls constantly coming in. "Sir," a specialist rushed to Lester. "The media is begging to know what's going on. We need to tell them something."

"Have all the parents of the children been notified already?" Lester asked.

"Yes. We informed them about everything as soon as the report was sent to us. What next?"

Lester nodded. "As long as the parents know, we can tell the media everything they want to know."

*****

The newscaster from New York News Channel Five came back on with a live report. "We have breaking news confirming the situation on the ISS. Our team is being told it's a cooling system malfunction. Launch Command in Houston has told us that the astronauts and cosmonauts are currently working on the problem."

*****

The parents were taken out of the lodging where they

were staying and brought over to the conference room where John, Galen, and Sharon sat at a long table. The parents sat across from them. Lester Jacobs walked into the room not long after. "I know you are all concerned about what's going on. Of course, I am too. There seems to be a problem on the ISS with the coolant system and it caused the communication systems to overheat as well as other things on board that shut down other systems."

Brandon's father slammed his fits on the table. "THINGS? OUR CHILDREN ARE IN DANGER ONBOARD YOUR ISS AND YOU SAY THINGS STOPPED WORKING! DON'T YOU HAVE A NAME FOR THESE SO-CALLED THINGS?"

Mukesh's father was next to speak. "Wait, are you trying to tell us there's no way for us to communicate with our children? And there's no way for you to know what's going on up there without any way to report back and forth? My son is up there not knowing if he's ever going to talk to us, his parents, again!"

"If everyone could please calm down for a moment and let me finish," Lester continued. "I know this is a very troubling situation. To answer your question, we can't communicate with them at the current moment. We are, however, able to monitor certain aspects of the ISS. That's how we were able to tell it was the coolant system that overheated."

"Please," Galen joined in the conversation. "Your children are in good hands with the astronauts and cosmonauts. They are highly trained and I'm sure they are working on a way to fix the problem."

"I know none of you will be sleeping tonight until we get news and that is why we are going to let you all stay here in the room if you'd like," Sharon stood up. "It's going to be a long night."

"As soon as we hear from the ISS, I will be back with an update," Lester said before leaving the conference room.

The parents sat in fear trying to take in all the news. They felt helpless knowing their children were in danger and there wasn't anything they could do sitting here at Strato-Labs headquarters.

*****

After trying to unsuccessfully pry open the door, the astronauts were able to grab the attention of the kids through the glass door. "What's going on?" Mukesh asked as Sumit guided him over to the group.

"It looks like Cal is holding up a grease board for us to read from," Sumie said. "It says the coolant system has malfunctioned. We believe the flow control valve needs to be replaced." She took a moment to catch her breath as Cal wiped away at the sign and wrote the next part. "The coolant control valve access door is on the outside of the ISS in the starboard pump module. The replacement valve and the exterior spacesuits are in your capsule. One of you will need to replace that valve."

Brandon looked over at the other kids. "But what about the exterior access door? If we can't open these doors, how will we open that one?"

"Good question," Amondi said grabbing a pen and paper. She wrote Brandon's question and put it against the glass for Cal to read.

Cal took his grease board and wrote out the answer. Sumie took charge of reading it to Mukesh. "Cal says there is a solar panel on the exterior side of the station. It's right next to the door that stores power in case of a situation such as this."

"Can I borrow that pen and paper?" Rafi asked Amondi. She handed it to him and Rafi wrote a message. "Sumie, please read this out loud so Mukesh can hear it too," he smiled.

"Maybe they should've thought about that for these doors as well."

All the kids nodded in agreement as Rafi showed the paper to the astronauts, causing Cal to smile. He wrote another message on his grease board: **Maybe you should work for NASA.**

Chapter 16

Panic reached Launch Command in Houston once the parents left the conference room. Galen looked at Lester and Sharon for answers. As a father to a boy only a couple of years older than the winners, he could imagine what the parents were going through at this time.

"Can't you send an emergency response team up there? Surely, you must've thought of something like that in case anything this severe happened," Galen questioned. He wanted to find a way to get the kids back down from the ISS and be here with their parents.

"There isn't enough time," Lester shook his head watching the monitors.

"What do you mean there isn't enough time? What do you suppose we tell the parents who entrusted their kids to us? We led them to believe their children would be safe on the ISS!"

"Galen, look at what it says on the control panel. There are only forty-five minutes left of oxygen. If we sent a response team, it would take them at least an hour to prepare the rocket and by then it would be too late. Listen, this is my company. I'm as responsible as you are if anything happens to those children. I'm doing everything possible to get them back home safe and sound."

"Don't you have an escape plan for times like this?" Sharon walked over to the two men.

"Yes, but the escape capsules aren't accessible because the coolant system turned the power off. I hate to say this, but this is a case of wait and see while trying to do anything to fix it."

*****

Brandon was remaining calm. He could see the look of fear in the faces of some of his fellow contestants. "Alright, we need to do what Cal said. Is there anyone who has a mechanical background?" he took charge.

"Me," Mukesh answered.

"You. But you're..." Rafi began but Mukesh cut him off.

"Yes, I know. I'm blind. My father is a mechanical engineer and he taught me how to repair items by feel. Since this is a little more serious, I can work with one of you and walk you through what we have to do."

"You can't feel through your space gloves though," Rafi pointed out. Mukesh nodded. He was right. "Now what?" Rafi through his hands in the air.

"Wait, someone can go with him," Amondi suggested.

"I will," Brandon volunteered. He walked over to guide Mukesh when an automated voice was heard over the speaker.

"Coolant level is now twenty percent. I repeat, coolant level is twenty percent."

86

*****

Later that evening, the parents were brought back to the conference room at Strato-Labs. Sumie's mother handed a tissue to Amondi's mother, both wiping their tears. Since the last time they were gathered, there had been no news. Now that they were all called back, the parents assumed the worst.

"You know what," Sumie's mother dried her eyes. "They're all smart kids. If my daughter was to be in a situation such as this, I'm glad she's with those she made friends with since we got here. I have a feeling they might be able to get out of this on their own."

"I feel the same way,' Amondi's mother agreed.

*****

The children on the ISS prepared to get ready to fix the valve the way Cal instructed. Sumie went off to find the replacement valve while Mukesh and Brandon went to go put on their spacesuits. "Guys," Mukesh called them over as he held a spacesuit next to his body. "Look, I know I might not be able to see, but even I can tell this is too large for me to wear."

"Not a problem," Genevieve opened a drawer, where they had placed their personal belongings. She opened up a case to reveal a portable sewing machine. "I've come prepared."

"That's what you chose as your one item to bring?" Rafi chuckled.

"Hey, it's going to help isn't it," she smiled at Rafi. "You're welcome." She grabbed both spacesuits and measured them against the two boys to know what size they needed. She didn't want to spend too much time working on them, knowing their time was precious and they needed to get the valve replaced.

Once Genevieve made the alterations, Amondi brought their portable air tanks to them. "They're all good to go." She turned to the glass door and gave a thumbs up to Cal.

Cal nodded. He looked at Commander Vacarr as he wrote something on the greaseboard and held it up. "I'll read to you what he says to do," Sumie said. "The map needed to locate the pump module is on the ISS tablet. Everything you need is there."

Amondi held the tablet while Rafi handed Brandon the new valve. "Here's the headsets for us to communicate with. I'm surprised they work."

"Yes, but they won't for long. We'll have to hurry," Brandon said.

Mukesh bent down and hugged Sumit. "Rafi, if I don't make it back, please take care of Sumit for me."

"I promise. But don't worry about that. The two of you will fix the valve and will come back to us," Rafi reassured them.

Brandon nodded and grabbed Mukesh's arm as the doors

opened to space.

*****

While the kids were trying their best to remain calm, it was a chaotic scene at Launch Command. They still couldn't communicate with the kids and the media was constantly calling for an update. They couldn't sugarcoat it anymore and had to tell the reporters the truth, which wasn't much. They were doing as much as they could.

Chapter 17

Brandon led the way, holding on to Mukesh's arm, placing his hand on the exterior panel. "It's right here," Brandon informed him.

"That's convenient," Mukesh answered.

Brandon looked over Mukesh's shoulder and saw Earth down below. "You and I are on a spacewalk. That's pretty cool when you think about it, am I right? No kid our age has ever done this before."

Mukesh smiled, "Yes, it is."

"Okay Mukesh, first, we open the panel with the screwdriver. We have to be careful not to lose any of the titanium screws."

*****

Launch Control was at a complete panic state as the control panel alerted them that the coolant level was at ten percent. There wasn't enough time left and they had to prepare an emergency launch for Strato-2000. "All prepared?" Lester asked as his workers nodded. He was hoping it wouldn't come down to this, but he couldn't sit back and not doing anything. He owed it to the parents to at least try and get their kids back. "Alright, let's do this and hope we aren't bringing bodies back home."

*****

Brandon and Mukesh worked feverishly on replacing the valve. "Okay, so the panel is off. Next, attach the coupling on that side. While you do that, I'll attach one on this side."

"Great." Brandon looked at the ISS tablet, "Now I'll open the bypass valve and it should be…" lights started to flicker on the panel and Brandon couldn't hold in how happy he was.

"IT'S WORKING!" Rafi shouted as the lights started to flicker on inside the ISS. The glass door separating the kids from the astronauts finally opened. Cal was the first one to join the kids in their room. "Well done!" he congratulated them. Now let's get the boys in here."

Chapter 18

Launch Command watched as the Strato-2000 emergency rocket launched. No one said a word, but they were all hoping for the same result, that the kids were fine and unharmed. The room was silent until Sharon noticed a light blinking on the control panel.

"They did it!" Sharon exclaimed. "They did it!"

"Yes, the emergency launch happened. Now, we have to hope for the best," Lester shook his head worriedly. Though this was chosen as a last resort, he feared it would be too late.

"No, Lester. I mean look," she pointed at the control panel. "The levels are going up. I don't know how they did it, but they managed to fix the problem."

Without waiting for another word, she nodded at Galen and they barged into the room where the parents sat. "The levels are all going up!" she announced. "Now, we're just waiting for word from the ISS that everything will be smooth sailing from now on. And hopefully, we'll soon be able to bring your children back home."

No other words were needed to be said as the parents cried tears of joy and hugged one another. Their children were safe and alive. That's all that mattered.

*****

Mukesh and Brandon arrived back inside the ISS where the other contestants waited for them. Rafi floated over, helping the two of them out of their exterior spacesuits and helmets. "You guys did it! You saved the day!" he patted them on their backs. "It must've been incredible being out there in space!"

"I think I would've enjoyed it more if it wasn't a matter of life or death," Brandon laughed. He put his hand on Mukesh's shoulder as they joined in with the other astronauts and cosmonauts in the room. "We made a good team."

"Yes, we did," Mukesh reached out to hug Brandon.

*****

"Finally, some good breaking news tonight with the ISS situation," the reporter appeared on television. Strato-Labs has sent us word that two of the winning contestants, Brandon and Mukesh, have completed a successful spacewalk, fixing the problem that occurred onboard the ISS. They replaced a coolant valve that compromised the oxygen and electricity levels. Our very own Jace Reynolds is over at headquarters now where they are preparing for a live feed from the ISS."

"Hi everyone," Jace said into the camera. It has been quite a crazy day here at Strato-Labs. For hours, we thought we would be reporting horrible news at the end of the night. But now we know, that isn't the case. We're waiting right now for Chief Jacobs to start the live feed where we will see the kids for the first time since they arrived in space."

Jace moved out of the way so his cameraman could focus on the front of the conference room where Lester was contacting the kids.

"This is Launch Command. Can you hear us?" one of Lester's men called up to the ISS.

"Yes. Loud and clear. This is Commander Vacarr speaking."

"Great," Lester joined in. "First, I want to congratulate Mukesh and Brandon on a job well done. Congratulations! You two showed extreme signs of bravery doing a spacewalk at your young ages. Your parents are here and watching this." The two boys smiled and waved at the camera when a sound was heard, causing everyone to jump. Lester turned to the parents. "No need to be alarmed, that's actually a good sound. That would be the Strato-2000 emergency rocket about to arrive at the ISS to bring the children all back to Earth."

"Oh man," Rafi stomped his foot. "I thought we'd all get a chance to do a spacewalk," he frowned.

Mukesh hugged his dog, Sumit. "Looks like we'll all be going home soon."

Chapter 19

earing they would be returning home to their parents was music to the kids' ears. While they thought that traveling to space was fabulous, after what they'd been through, they were ready to go home. The astronauts helped them prepare for Strato-2000 to arrive.

"I'm really going to miss all of you," Cal told the kids. "I know it wasn't long, but you six are really smart. I hope to see you all working for NASA or Strato-Labs one day." A sound went off and the hatch opened. "That's for you. I know your parents will be happy to see you all again."

The children waved to the astronauts and cosmonauts before entering the Strato-2000. A short time later, they returned back to Earth. After being checked out by a NASA doctor, all six kids were given the 'all clear'. They walked into headquarters where their parents waited for their arrival. After their ordeal, the kids wanted to go home and be with their parents, but the reporters had other ideas.

The reporters all made a beeline to the children when Sharon and Galen stepped in front of them. "Please, they just arrived back to Earth and want to be with their parents. Give them a few minutes," Galen said.

Jace wasn't having any of it. He wanted to be the first reporter to get an interview with the children. He snuck past Galen and Sharon and walked over to the group of kids. "We all want to know, how does it feel being back home?"

Brandon smiled, "I was excited to go to space but I'm more excited to be back on Earth."

"It feels wonderful!" Genevieve said. "I can finally get rid of this jumpsuit with orange stripes and never have to worry about wearing it again. It clashed with my hair and skin. Did you know notice that?"

Jace laughed at her statement. "What about you?" he asked Rafi. "You made us laugh with your comments before you took off."

"I try," Rafi blushed and laughed. "What you saw was me just being well...me. I'm a clown, I'll admit that. First, let me say that I'm upset that I never got to take a spacewalk and never was able to perform some space magic. Brandon and Mukesh told us how amazing it was and I'll admit, I was jealous at first that I didn't get to do it. But then I remembered the reason why they did it was to save us. If I was to go out with them, I probably would've frozen and wouldn't be much help. What does matter is the fact that I made great friends within the past three weeks."

"Thank you so much for the interview. I don't want to keep you from your parents any longer. They spent enough time away from you. Let me say it's great to have you all back here."

Brandon, Genevieve, and Rafi walked back to where the other three contestants were with their parents. Six different children from all corners of the globe came together because of one common interest, their love of space exploration. And though they had their differences, whether it was being blind, or just being goofy to make everyone laugh, they soon learned that it was those differences that made them friends.

Together, they answered a few more questions from other reporters before Sharon made the announcement that it was time to allow the children to leave with their parents. With a wave, they walked out of Strato-Labs headquarters happy to be back home.

THE END

ABOUT THE AUTHOR

Joe Palumbo is a screenwriter, novelist and cinematographer. He lives in Burlington, Vermont.